Brainy Bot belongs to:

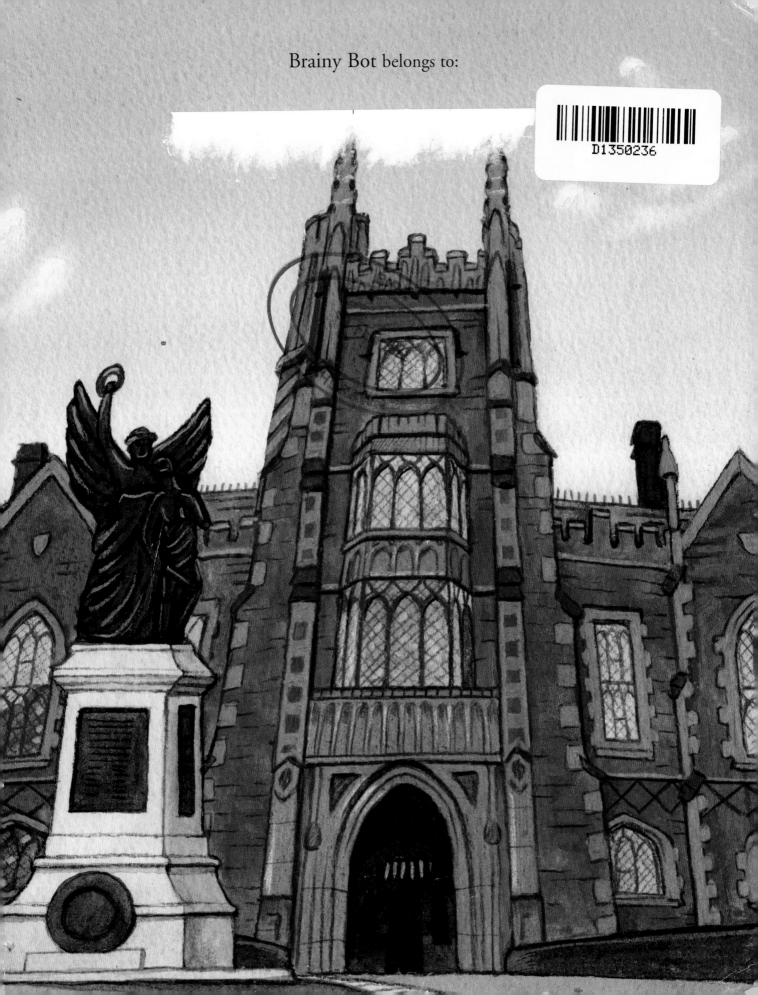

For Mum with love
- L.G.

For Joseph, Jack, Bella & Luan
- D.O.

For Rachael O'Donnell
- B.O'D.

Text copyright © 2009 Lauren Graham
Illustrations copyright © 2009 Dave Orchard

First published in Ireland by O'Donnell Press 2009
12 Coolemoyne Park, Jordanstown, Co. Antrim BT37 0RP
Telephone: 028 9096 6493
Email: b.odonnell93@ntlworld.com
www.odonnellpress.com

Special thanks to Paul Porter.

A CIP catalogue record of this book is available from the British Library.

Printed in Ireland by GPS Colour Graphics Ltd.

ISBN 978-0-9553325-8-6

1 2 3 4 5 6 7 8 9 10

 O'DONNELL PRESS

Brainy Bot

The South Belfast Squirrel

By Lauren Graham

Illustrated by Dave Orchard

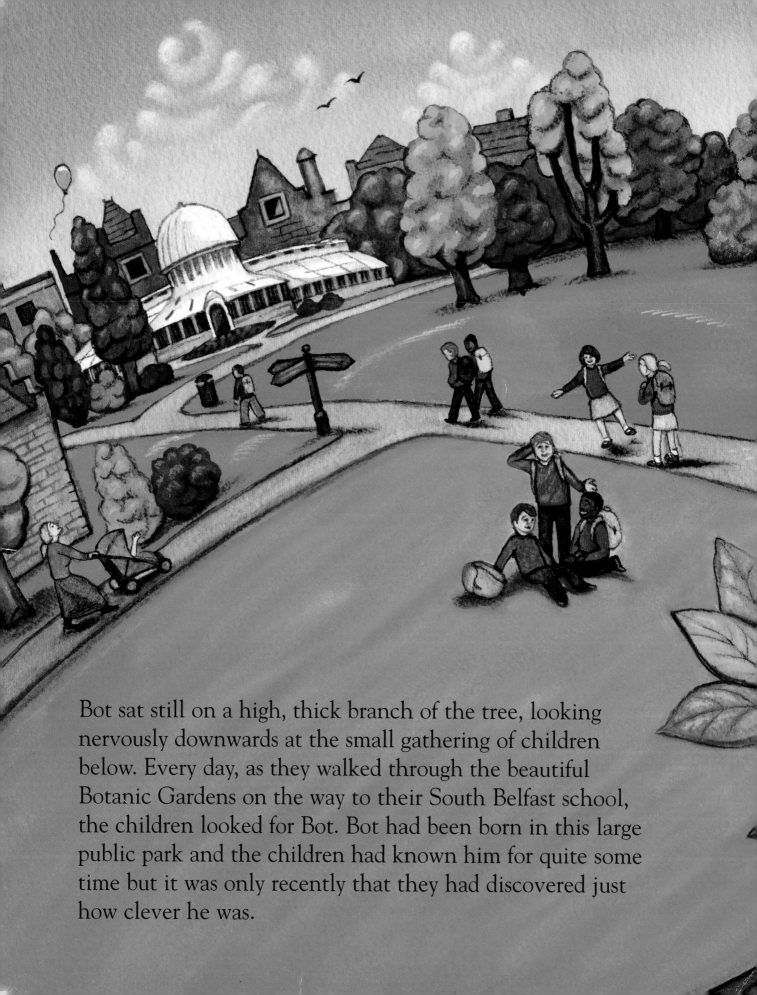

Bot sat still on a high, thick branch of the tree, looking nervously downwards at the small gathering of children below. Every day, as they walked through the beautiful Botanic Gardens on the way to their South Belfast school, the children looked for Bot. Bot had been born in this large public park and the children had known him for quite some time but it was only recently that they had discovered just how clever he was.

Some weeks earlier, Charles and Carmel had been relaxing in the sunshine on one of the grassy banks in the middle of the park. They were trying to remember the number facts for their test the following day. "What is the total of seven and three?" asked Charles. Just as Carmel was about to answer, the children noticed Bot running backwards and forwards across the grass in front of them, carrying acorns in his front paws. He set the acorns down in two little piles. As the children watched in amazement, they realised that the first little pile contained seven acorns, the other one had three. Bot was helping them with their number facts. "Brainy Bot, Brainy Bot!" the children cried with glee, jumping up and down with excitement.

News of the smart squirrel soon spread and children began flocking to the park in an eager attempt to catch a glimpse of Brainy Bot. As his popularity grew, the children began to make up rhymes about him. "Bot is brilliant, Bot is bright. He counts acorns and gets it right!"

A few days later, the children again spotted Bot.
This time he was following some tourists through the
Palm House that is located in the middle of the park.
He was trying to learn about the tropical plants that
grow there. "Look, look!" the children cried, "Brainy
Bot is in the dome!" and they began a new chant.
"Bot is brilliant, Bot is bright. He knows that tropical
plants need warmth and light!"

It was very windy the next day. Carmel had taken her kite to fly it in the park. She was having fun. Suddenly, a gust of wind yanked the kite from her hand. Bot had been watching Carmel from his favourite spot on the branch of a tall tree. Realising what had happened, he ran down the tree towards the kite. As he stretched forward and his front paw touched the string, the other children appeared.

"Look, look!" they yelled, "Brainy Bot is holding the kite!" and they started to call out a new chant.

"Bot is brilliant, Bot is bright. He can even fly a kite!"

Early in the morning, a few days later, as the Ulster Museum was just opening its doors, Bot slipped unseen through the entrance and up the stairs. This was not his first time in the museum. He was a frequent visitor, for he wanted to learn as much as he could about the exhibits that were stored inside. On this particular morning, his plan was to visit Takabuti, the Egyptian mummy. Charles was also paying a visit to the museum.
As Charles entered the Egyptian room, he caught sight of Bot hiding behind one of the glass display cabinets. "Look, look! It's Brainy Bot!" he shouted. As soon as Bot realised that he had been spotted, he bolted out of the room, jumped through an open window onto a branch of a nearby tree and was gone in a flash.

EGYPTIAN ROOM

Takabuti. 760BC

Charles could hardly contain his excitement. He couldn't wait to meet up with his friends to tell them the latest news about Brainy Bot.

Later, as Charles and his friends ran through the park, they chanted, "Bot is brilliant, Bot is bright. He knows Takabuti is wrapped up tight!"

Bot was beginning to get quite big-headed with all this attention. He wanted to show the children just how clever he really was, so he came up with a plan that was sure to impress them. The next day, he left the Botanic Gardens and scurried off to the nearby Queen's University.

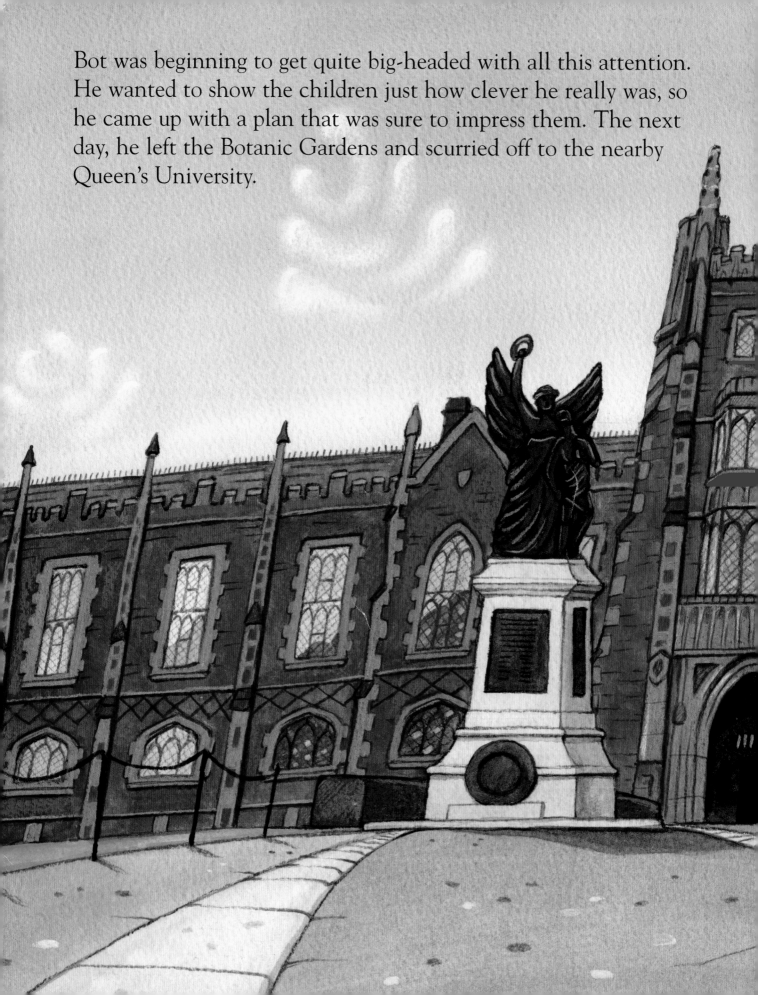

On warm, sunny days, he had seen many of the students from Queen's working in the gardens and knew that they were very knowledgeable. The University library was just the right place for Bot to learn something new.

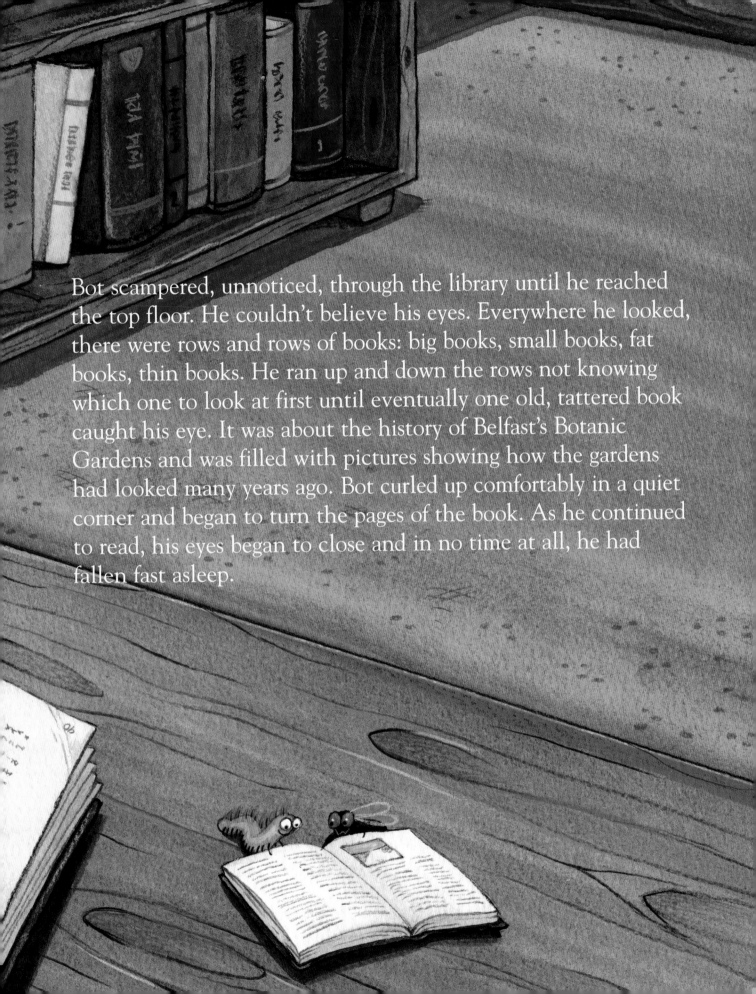

Bot scampered, unnoticed, through the library until he reached the top floor. He couldn't believe his eyes. Everywhere he looked, there were rows and rows of books: big books, small books, fat books, thin books. He ran up and down the rows not knowing which one to look at first until eventually one old, tattered book caught his eye. It was about the history of Belfast's Botanic Gardens and was filled with pictures showing how the gardens had looked many years ago. Bot curled up comfortably in a quiet corner and began to turn the pages of the book. As he continued to read, his eyes began to close and in no time at all, he had fallen fast asleep.

When he awoke, the library was
dark and silent. Everyone had
gone home and Bot was locked
inside. He rushed around
frantically, looking for a way out.
There was no escape. Upset and
frightened, he slipped back into
the quiet corner and lay very still,
waiting for his opportunity to
escape. When the librarian
opened up the following morning,
a bushy tail brushed by her legs
and she watched as a small, scared
squirrel fled quickly away in the
direction of the Botanic Gardens.

Of course, it wasn't long before everyone knew about the library's overnight visitor. As soon as the children heard, they were sure that the little squirrel in the library just had to be Brainy Bot. They hunted for Bot in the gardens and after a while found him resting on his favourite branch. The children skipped and played on the grass below, singing yet another new chant, "Bot is brilliant, Bot is bright. He reads in the library all through the night!" Bot knew that this was one chant that certainly wasn't quite correct but being such a smart, sensible squirrel, he decided to keep the truth about his night in the library all to himself.

However, being locked in the library did teach Bot a valuable lesson. His big-headedness had landed him in trouble and he would never again be so full of himself.

As he sat motionless on the high, thick branch of his favourite tree, looking timidly downwards at the small gathering of children below, Bot now knew that the safest place for a South Belfast squirrel was high among the trees in the Botanic Gardens. The brainiest choice he could ever make would be to never leave this beautiful park again.

Enjoy more great picture books from
O'Donnell Press

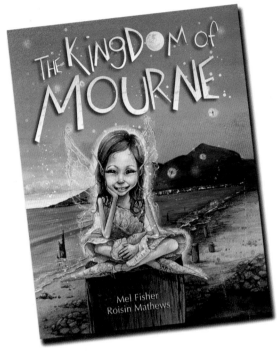

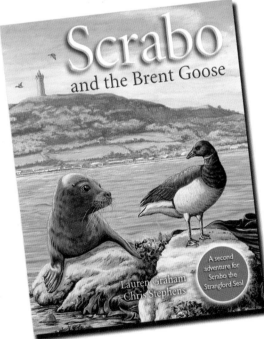

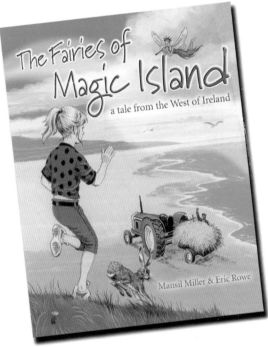

Visit: www.odonnellpress.com